Emma Rides
on the Erie Canal

by Tracy Zimmerman
illustrated by Ralph Canaday

 HOUGHTON MIFFLIN   BOSTON

Little Falls, New York

Emma was so excited she could not stand still. Today, September 3, 1871, she would take her first ride on the Erie Canal. She had been waiting for this day for what seemed like forever.

Ever since she could remember, Emma had heard of the wondrous things the canal had made possible. Before the Erie Canal was built, travel west of the Allegheny Mountains had been difficult and dangerous. But the canal, a channel four feet deep, had changed people's lives dramatically. It was 363 miles long and stretched from Buffalo, New York, on the far western border of the state, to Troy, on the far eastern side.

Boats of many kinds could now move both people and goods easily from the Great Lakes all the way to New York City, and much more quickly than on land. Just the year before, Emma's neighbors, the Wackers, had joined the thousands of settlers who used the Erie Canal to move from the East to farms and towns on the frontier. By traveling on the canal, the Wackers had avoided the dirt roads that changed from an ocean of mud to an endless chain of baked ruts as spring turned into summer each year.

Standing on deck, Emma watched as passengers came on board and goods for trade were loaded, including livestock. She heard whistles, shouting, and all kinds of commotion. Families climbed on with their possessions. Cattle mooed as their owners prodded, pushed, and tugged them aboard. Chickens squawked in crates. Some people stooped and staggered under the weight of heavy sacks.

Emma's father and her big brother, Sam, hauled barrels of potatoes on deck. Her father was transporting the potatoes to sell in Troy. Some he had grown on their farm, and some he was selling for neighbors. The whole family was along, including Emma's younger brother, Nick. The trip from Little Falls to Troy, a distance of more than eighty miles, would take all day.

Emma and Nick explored the crowded, noisy boat. It looked like a flatboat with two small cabins on top—narrow, and about as long as their barn. On the canal banks they could see shops, stores, houses among the trees, people hurrying on errands, and horses nibbling grass.

Emma was anxious to get under way. "Mama, when do we go?" she asked impatiently.

"Once everything's loaded," Mama answered.

Emma looked around her at dozens of other boats. "What are they all doing?" she asked.

Papa nodded toward a low, flat boat. "That barge is carrying lumber." He pointed to another. "That one's a blunt-nosed barge called a laker. It could be carrying grain. Some people go from place to place selling medicine. I've even seen dancing bears on the canal!" Papa winked at her.

Finally their boat began to move. Soon it passed a small boat moored on the side of the canal. The boat looked like a shack on a raft, with peeling paint and rusting metal parts. "That's a shanty boat," Papa said quietly. "A family lives inside."

A little farther along, the canal boat drifted slowly toward the bank, and another boat passed it. Ladies and gentlemen in elegant clothes lounged about, enjoying the sunshine on the boat's deck, and Emma and Nick waved to them. "Why are they going faster than us?" Emma asked.

"They have a lighter load. Those people are on a packet boat, and they're traveling just for fun," Papa said. "A packet boat carries only passengers with hand luggage, not freight like ours. We're traveling at about four miles an hour, but packet boats often go six or seven miles an hour. They have the right of way, which means that they get to go ahead of any boats that are moving more slowly."

"Emma, come watch the steersman!" Nick called. Emma ran to the back of the boat. There they watched a man steer the boat by moving a big rudder with a long wooden handle called a tiller.

"Low bridge! Everybody down!" the steersman shouted suddenly. On the wooden bridge ahead Emma saw a farm wagon crossing. The bridge was so low that when the canal boat passed underneath, passengers had to bend or crouch near the deck—or risk being swept overboard. Just then, Emma noticed her mischievous brother Sam. He was jogging alongside the boat!

"Papa, what is Sam doing on the land?"

Sam had leaped off the boat when no one was looking and was bounding onto the bridge up ahead. Just as the canal boat passed under the bridge, Sam jumped the few feet from the bridge to the cabin with a thud, like a mountain goat. He was grinning broadly. Papa glared in disapproval. Emma was annoyed. She thought Sam took too many chances in his merrymaking.

There was so much to see on the journey! Carpenters were building new houses near the canal. Sounds of hammers pounding and workers shouting filled the air. The canal boat drifted on, past villages, swamps, fields, and patches of forest. Emma had rarely traveled away from her family's farm, and then only to go to town in the wagon.

High hills rose ahead as the canal boat approached a lock and glided to a stop. Emma's father explained how the lock worked. From the western end of the Erie Canal to the eastern end, the land fell 565 feet, so the boats traveling eastward had to go "downhill." Eighty-three locks, built in different spots along the canal, made the descent easier. Each lock was like a room that would hold only one boat at a time. When the boat pulled into the lock, watertight doors on either end closed. Then, water was drained from the lock until the water level reached the level of the next portion of the canal. Finally, the doors on the lower level opened, and the boat could move on its way.

Boats going westward on the canal would pass through the locks in the other direction as they traveled "uphill." Each lock would be filled with water, lifting the boats up to the next level of the canal.

As the canal boat was being prepared to enter the lock, some passengers disembarked and wandered along the bank, while others stepped into a dry goods store on the shore. "This may take a while," Mama said. "We'll eat lunch and just wait until the water level is low enough that our boat can continue down the canal."

Although she was hungry, Emma frowned at the delay. She enjoyed floating along on the water and looking at the scenery and activity on the shore. But Mama seemed to read Emma's mind. She reached into a bag and pulled out a package wrapped in plain brown paper. "This may help you pass the time," Mama said. "I've been saving it for a special occasion."

Emma tore open the package. It was a book—not just any book, but *Folktales from Around the World*. Numerous times she had admired the gold lettering on its handsome red cover in a store in Little Falls. "Oh, thank you, Mama!" Emma exclaimed. She opened the cover carefully.

For an hour after lunch, Emma leaned against a barrel on the deck near the front of the boat, devouring page after page of her new book. She read about the doomed prince of Egypt. She read about England's famous Robin Hood. She read Amazon legends from South America and tales about Russian kings. She didn't notice that the boat had started moving again until a shadow fell across her lap. Looking up, she saw Sam standing with his hands behind his back. His grin told Emma that once again he was up to no good. "Look what I found," he said, revealing what he was holding. It was a beautiful rag doll, carefully sewn by hand of cotton cloth and thread, with embroidered eyebrows, eyes, nose, and mouth, and dark brown string for hair. Emma's best friend, Margaret, had let Emma borrow it for the trip. Sam must have found it among the things Emma brought on board the boat.

"Give that back right this minute!" Emma cried. She sprang to her feet, still clutching her new book. But Sam was backing away from her with the doll.

Emma was furious. She grabbed wildly for the doll. Sam backed farther away, then jumped onto a barrel near the side of the boat. Emma stepped onto a box beside the barrel. She grabbed Sam's leg and reached for the doll again.

Suddenly, Sam jumped down and ran off with the doll. Emma lost her balance on the box and tumbled to the deck of the boat, but the book slipped from her grasp. With a gasp of horror, she saw the book drop out of sight into the murky water of the canal. The book had fallen overboard!

At Emma's cries for help, both her parents came running, along with the skipper of the boat. In tears, Emma explained what had happened and pointed to the spot where the book had disappeared. The skipper whistled to another crewman near the front of the boat, who quickly brought a large net attached to a long handle. The two men ran toward the rear.

"The book will be nearly behind us now, but if we're lucky we might still reach it with this," the skipper said as he lowered the net into the water off the back of the boat. Emma held her breath, wondering if she would ever see the book again. The skipper's first attempt was unsuccessful. But as he pulled the net up on his second try, Emma glimpsed something red in the net. It was her book!

The skipper fished the book from the net and placed it in Emma's hands. The book was soaked with water and stained with mud. It would never look new again.

"It's still in one piece," said Emma's mother gently. "We can dry the pages carefully, and you may still be able to read it."

For the rest of the afternoon, Emma didn't even look at Sam. She was too angry. Both children received a severe scolding, but Emma thought the accident was all Sam's fault. She stayed by herself on deck as long as she could, looking at the view.

Before reaching Schenectady, the boat came to an aqueduct that carried the Erie Canal like a bridge across the Mohawk River. The sun was setting on the water, which wound through the valley like a ribbon. As the canal boat eased around a bend, Emma looked back and counted the stone piers supporting the long aqueduct. How strange, she thought, that one stream of water could be made to flow above another!

At suppertime, Mama got out the picnic hamper again. There were sweet potato biscuits—Emma's favorite. Sam handed Emma an extra biscuit. "Sorry, sis," he mumbled. Emma munched on the biscuit, still unable to reply. Maybe, she thought—just maybe—Sam wasn't such a monster after all.

When the sun went down, the family rested in the cabin. Emma watched the sunset through the cabin door. The sky darkened from lavender to deepest blue, and a half moon hung just above the trees. By the time they reached Troy, Emma was almost asleep. She had had more than enough excitement for her first day on the Erie Canal.